This book belongs to:

First published in Great Britain in 2011 by Andersen Press Ltd.,

20 Vauxhall Bridge Road, London SW1V 2SA.

Published in Australia by Random House Australia Pty.,

Level 3, 100 Pacific Highway, North Sydney, NSW 2060.

Text and Illustration copyright © Michael Foreman, 2011

The rights of Michael Foreman to be identified as the

author and illustrator of this work have been asserted by him

in accordance with the Copyright, Designs and Patents Act, 1988.

All rights reserved.

Colour separated in Switzerland by Photolitho AG, Zürich.

Printed and bound in Singapore by Tien Wah Press.

Michael Foreman has used watercolour and pastels in this book.

10   9   8   7   6   5   4   3   2   1

British Library Cataloguing in Publication Data available.

ISBN 978 1 84939 323 2 (hardback)

ISBN 978 1 84939 383 6 (paperback)

This book has been printed on acid-free paper

Oh! If Only...

MICHAEL FOREMAN

ANDERSEN PRESS

Oh! If only . . .

I had stayed at home that day . . .

If only ... I hadn't met that dog ...

If only ... he didn't have that ball ...

If only . . . he didn't want to play . . .

If only . . . I was better at football
and hadn't tried to show off . . .

If only . . . the ball hadn't bounced down the hill . . .

And, **if** only . . . the dog hadn't chased after it

and frightened the old lady's cats . . .

who frightened the birds . . .

who spooked the horses . . .

who wrecked . . . the BIG PARADE . . .

and ruined the QUEEN'S BIRTHDAY!

And, if only . . .
the dog hadn't continued
to chase the ball . . .

past all the sentries and the servants . . .

through the Palace and out again, wrecking the carpets . . .

and knocking over the birthday cake and lots of fancy stuff . . .

Oh! And if only...

he hadn't brought the ball back to *me* . . .

in front of all the world's TV cameras . . .

Oh! If only I had stayed home that day . . .

I wouldn't be the most embarrassed person in the

WHOLE WIDE WORLD!

BUT . . .

If I had stayed at home that day . . .

I would never have met this great dog!

Other books illustrated by Michael Foreman:

9781849392242

9781842705827

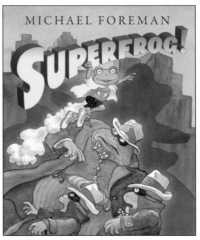

9781849392099

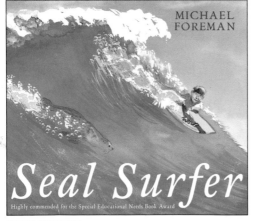

9781842705780

9781842704486

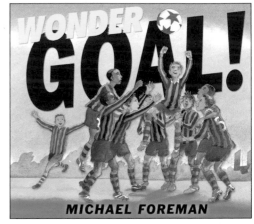

9781842709344